Rocky's Road to the Big City

Written by Jessica DelVirginia
Illustrated by Courtney Ling

My name is Rocky, and I am a Saw-whet owl. Everyone thinks I'm a baby when they see me, but I'm just naturally small.

I like being shorter than my friends, because I can fit into smaller hiding spaces when we play in the trees!

I live in Oneonta, New York. No, not the city, but it turns out that I do have a funny story about that.

My parents named me Rocky. I am the colors of the natural rocks and stones near where I hatched.

I want to tell you about a time when
my life was changed forever. Growing
up, I would always see the neighbor
humans putting sparkles on the small
trees near their houses. They always
did this when it got cold in the winter.

It seemed silly, because the sparkles
would only last a short amount of
time. But it gave us owls an extra
place to perch and feel warm from
the light. I liked them.

It was starting to get colder, and I just knew in my feathers that the humans would start hanging the sparkles soon.

I cuddled up against the big tree I was living in and went to sleep.

I woke up to a rumble, but was too scared to fly away.

As I sat on my branch, I felt the tree rocking back and forth, and got a little dizzy.

The next thing I knew, the tree went down with a big whoosh, and landed with a thump and a cloud of dust. I must have hit my head, because it made me take a nap.

HOO   HOO

HELLO

I woke up to a very strong wind and loud rumbling, but I was in the dark.

"Hello? Who's there?" I managed to shout.

No one heard me. The rumbling continued for what felt like days.

Suddenly, the darkness went away. I could see morning light. I was a little squished in the branches, but it felt almost cozy.

I began to hear humans again, and they sounded like they were working hard.

Suddenly, my branch moved, and one human looked me straight in the face.

"Hey guys, come look at this baby owl."

I wanted to protest, "I'm not a baby!" but no noise came out.

This human was different. He had a something covering his mouth, and his hands were green and felt warm when he picked me up. I was scared, and I was so hungry.

The masked human put me in a box with a blanket and branches, and then more rumbling started. I was still hungry, so I was getting grumpy. I scowled at him.

When the rumbling stopped, the human took me and my box inside a building. I had never been in one of those!

Another human looked at me and immediately brought me some yummy mice.

While I was in the new human's building, a magic picture box on the wall was showing the tree I grew up in. But the tree wasn't where it usually was. It was by a frozen pond, a big, golden, shiny human, and lots of tall buildings! And, the tree was covered in a million sparkles!

The humans in the box were talking about a baby owl that caught a ride to "the city" with the tree.

I looked close at the picture box. That baby owl looked like me, from all the times I had seen my reflection in a window.

Then, they showed the human who found me!

They were talking about me. But they were wrong. I'm not a baby!

The human on the picture box said, "They've decided to call her Rockefeller, Rocky for short."

I thought, 'How do they know my name?'

The human turned to me and said, "See Rocky, everyone knows about your journey. We're going to get you nice and strong so you can go on your way, back to your family and friends."

A few more fresh mouse meals later, the human took me back outside. It was colder than when we left my tree.

She put me on her hand, and off I flew! Back home to my friends and family. With stories to tell of the place with big buildings, gold human, and very few trees.

It was a cold-weather, sparkly-tree, miracle.

Made in the USA
Middletown, DE
04 December 2021

54021065R00015